DELIVARY GIRL

KABIR SINGH

ISBN 979-888569520-6

I dedicate this book to my friends and my parents. Those people have helped me a lot. I will be forever grateful to them.

Contents

Foreword

This book tells the story of a girl named Reena. And in this you get to know how truth prevails and how evil ends.

Preface

author kabir write this book for readers to know how evil get lost and a truth won the case . this story is a fication novel . all chrectrs and story is all auther's imagination .

Acknowledgements

i'm thanks full of my around peoples who help me emotional, moral, financial, or academic support while undertaking the challenge of writing a book.

Prologue

i know befor this you read severls of books like that but I promise after read this book you defiantly get an new test of reading so read and lost in this world .

seacion 1

mohan mathur

Indhar Mathur with his wife Susmita Mathur is watching prime time news on TV, keeping the other foot on one leg and moving the sheet till it kneads a bit. News Anker tells that his special guest today is Advocate Mohan Mathur. Mohan Mathur is known as the Bhahubali of the world of advocacy, because to date there was not a single case that could raise a finger on his advocacy. In whatever case comes inintois hands, the defense lawyer starts peeking in his black coat only after hearing Mathur's name. On hearing the name of Mohan Mathur from News Anker, Indhar Mathur lifts the TV remote kept on the nearby door and turns off the TV.

"Know what is it that you hate your father so much till today," Sushmita says while pulling the sheet on her with one hand and falling asleep on her side with the other side. Indhar Mathur does not say anything and puts the remote

back near the TV, opens the door, takes out a cigarette and lighter, and goes to the balcony. After a coffee cup time, Sushmita does not see Indhar on the bed, she also comes to the balcony without saying anything, keeping her hands on the front railing and looking at the vehicles passing below.

"What happened you are not sleeping?" Indhar asks Sushmita with the little left cigarette in his hand.

"No" Sushmita reply

"What happened to you? Why are you smoking a cigarette?

today at bedtime? As much as I know you, without any tension, you don't smoke cigarettes." Folding her hands on her chest, sushmitaasks to Mathur,

"Sukriya my dear wife for taking such care, and let me tell you that today your guess is completely wrong. I don't have any tension, that's why I wanted to smoke a cigarette" Indhar says while throwing the last piece of cigarette in the corner of the balcony.

"There is no need to show so much love, I know there is something you don't want to tell

me, and if you don't, don't tell,"

Sushmita tells Indhar to sleep and goes to bed. After two or three minutes, Indhar also falls asleep.

Mohan Mathur is Indhar Mathur's father but Indhar Mathur has not spoken to his father for lathe st 12 years. The reason for this hatred is "Bharti Mathur's death". Due to being in the car, the car overturned and that is why Bharti Mathur is not in this world today, it seems to Indhar Mathur that is why he hates his sin Mohan Mathur so much. And wherever he has a liver, Indhar Mathur leaves

immediately. And he has been hiding this thing from his wife Sushmita to date. Indhar Mathur once tried every day to prove himself better than him by helping his sin Mohan Mathur in some cases, but luck was not supporting him till now, his dream was still a dream. But that night when Indhar Mathur was preparing for some case, due to that some law books were kept on the table, and with one hand he was sitting near the window and the rain was also getting louder that night. Then his eyes fell on a delivery

scooter on the road below, a girl was sitting on it, the age would be about 23 or 24 years, she was constantly looking at Indhar Mathur and then suddenly disappeared. The book fell from Indhar Mathur's hand and his whole body was drenched in sweat. That night Indhar Mathur fell asleep and goes to court in the morning.

In the evening, when Indhar Mathur puts his car in the parking lot, goes to the lift to go to his flat which is on the third floor, and presses the button to open it, as soon as the door of

the lift opens, there was the same delivery girl in front. Was standing in that rain last night. Seeing him, Indgar Mathur starts going towards the side, only then the girl shouts "Work is going on that side, today you have to go by lift."

Indhar Mathur holds his brown leather bag tightly in both hands and says "Hmm". The tax goes to the lift. His blood was running as fast as a fighter jet. As soon as the lift opens up, Indhar Mathur comes out hurriedly and looks back with a little panic that the girl who was with him is

no longer there in the lift and then his eyes fell on a parcel lying in the lift. Goes near looks around and picks up the parcel. Change clothes quickly Indhar Mathur opens that parcel. and starts reading.

seaction

A year ago -

What's the matter son, after how many days you have worn this red T-shirt, I remember you wear this only when there is a special day, so tell me what is

the matter? Reena's father Kishore Das asks her

my friend, is his call, it was said that our high school results are going to come this evening, and this t-shirt is very lucky for me, that's why I wore it, Reena from her father says |

Kishore Das is a very punctual man of time, neither one minute ahead nor one minute behind. It is early morning and Kishore Das is getting ready to go to his shop. Wearing a white shirt and black pants every day, wears it like an office uniform and a tiffin in which parathas made by

Sarada ji's hands, which contain little ghee, because only two years ago he had heart oppression. So the doctor has asked to eat less fat.

Reena's mother Sarada Das is preparing breakfast in the kitchen and Reena is busy cleaning the house. There is no brother or sister and when Reena was born, the doctor had said that Sarada Das would not be able to become a mother anymore and if she still does this, then her life may be in danger, only then Kishore Das Ji had thought that a daughter is

enough, nowadays even having daughters is a matter of luck. Kishore Das also had a lot of respect due to the same thinking towards the society, look anywhere from the locality to the market, everyone calls him by saying only Kishore Ji and his wife Sarada Das is just like him when that too when someone is seen with low eyes. Only then does Reena dream of serving society by becoming a doctor.

After having breakfast, Kishore went to the shop and Reena's cleaning was also completed.

"Reena daughter, you can also have breakfast, it is hot now" Sarada Ji sounds from the kitchen inside,

"Ji, mom, just have to make a bed, then the work is done" Reena replies while fixing the bedsheet. If there is more work in the house in the morning, then Reena also gives her mother's hand.

The hand of the clock was showing the time of 3 o'clock and Reena's mother's phone was ringing. done |

"See what the result?" Bhavna asks

"No yaar"

"Tune" Reena asks Bhavna

Did you check"Yes I am second in class and you are first" Upon hearing this feeling, Reena choked saying "Really what"

"Bhavna said yes true Me" and then Reena's mother Sarada Das also reached there when Reena told that she has come first in the class, then her eyes filled with tears. Reena quickly made a call to her father Kishore Ji and told him about

the result. Everyone in the house seemed happy and the rest of the classmates were also calling and congratulating them. In the evening, Kishore Ji reaches home with a box of sweets and feeds Reena with his own hands.

Reena, "Papa you said that if the numbers are good then you will send me to NEET coaching and the time has come for you to fulfill your promise"

Kishore Das, "Yes, who is your son to you, doctor? Why not your father will help you my son"

Listening to her father's words, Reena says while hugging Kishore Das Ji with full eyes, "you are the best papa in the world"

everything was going well that suddenly around three to four nights Around o'clock, Reena's mother Sarada started getting chakras and started vomiting blood, Kishore Das had neither a vehicle nor a scooter, so Kishore Das called Ramkishan Ji to the neighborhood and took Sarada to the hospital. Seeing this, Reena started crying, she also came to the hospital with him and was sitting on the chair with Ramkishan Ji, inside KishoreJii was busy getting his tests done with Sarada Ji. Ramkishan Ji was comforting Reena that her mother had become completely teak so that Reena would stop crying. It was morning while circling the hospital, everyone was tired and there was a little eye waiting on the bench outside, only then the nurse's voice is heard, she was calling Kishore Das ji's name, listen to this Reena, Ramkishan Ji and Kishore Das All of them run away from him. The nurse told that the test report of Sarada Das has come. "What happened sister to him?" Kishore Das Ji asks the nurse

"brain tumor" The nurse dropped in a low voice. And everyone standing in front of them felt so heavy that their heart trembled, no one understood what to do. Reena ran towards Sarada ji's ward and started crying loudly while thrashing the door calling her mother. Both Kishore Das and Ramkishan Ji hugged Reena and started silencing her.

Ramkishan Ji took Raina out of the hospital and Kishore Das Ji started asking the doctor for the rest of the information.

The doctor told that Sarada Ji has only one or two weeks' time left, you should spend full time with her. Kishore Das, "No treatment is there, what is the doctor sir",

Doctor, "If we had, we would have told, but this is the last state, there is no" cure forand then the doctor leaves from there by saying let me go.

Kishore Das told Reena that her mother is fine and she will be allowed to go home from the hospital by tomorrow. Kishore Das did not want to make Reena sad by telling him that his mother has brain cancer and only a few suns remain in this world for his BS. Ramkishan Sharma Ji who came along had come to know the sadness on Kishore Das's face and he had an idea that something must be there or else Kishore Das, a man who laughs every day, would not be sad. But Reena was also

there, she could not ask anything from this idea. Tonight was to be spent in the hospital, so Kishore Das stopped there and Ramkishan Sharma came home with Reena. Reena's aunt, who lived a short distance away, had reached home as soon as she got the news. By noon, Kishore Das had also taken Sarada Das from the hospital to his house. Hearing the news of Sarada Das's illness, people from nearby also started coming to meet him. Neither Kishore had any younger brother and elder brother and

Reena's grandfather had passed away many years ago, so now all the responsibility in the house was under the control of Kishore Das.

Reena had given an exam for Dalkile in the medical college a few days ago, today her result was also announced, then Kishore Das got engaged in that work and on the other hand, the sun of Sarada Das's life was also near setting as per the doctor's advice.

A few days later........

today's sun had come out a bit different than the other days, neither was any bird screaming today nor was it a new dawn in the morning of the morning like every day. When Reena gets up from her bed, she sees that there are people everywhere in the house and everyone's eyes are moist like dew drops. Seeing Kishore Das, Reena also could not stop herself and her eyes started raining, till now she had known that her mother was not a part of this world, she

would never call her Reena daughter.

After a few more days, Reena still did not come out of her mother's sorrow, the smile on her face and the enthusiasm of becoming a doctor had been lost as soon as possible.

Then with the changing times, Reena had to burden herself with this sorrow, it was not as if she had forgotten her mother, but now she did not remember that much, the dust of time started sticking on those memories. Kishore Das also started going back to his shop,

both of them had once again returned to normal life and now Reena's aunt also started living in their house because her husband is not worried, nor does she have any children. Now Reena had considered herself as her daughter.

Now Reena had to go to college too, but Reena was not at all happy about this.

“Why are you sad Reena, college is a little far away from home, only 30 minutes is the way,” said Kishore Das, placing his hand on Reena’s head.

“And we will bring comfortably, you can also go to college”

a scooty, “Scooty”, Reena says with a little surprise

Is Kishore Das shaking his head a little “Why? Don’t want what?"

"Oh papa" saying so much, Reena hugs her father Kishore Das.

Today Reena has made potato parathas for dinner, they are eaten in breakfast, but Reena does not know how to make anything else, so she made this because today her aunt has also gone to her house.

“Wah wonderful, have you made parathas, son, it is absolutely the taste of your mother’s hands,” says Kishore Das, putting a morsel in his mouth.

Mother’s name heard Reena’s face turned sad watching these "teenage slave eating Speaking of keeping a strand Reina son you may also weaken Ase bids thee what will

Bude father Icon an honest singing"

little Eye The water flashes and then with a small smile, Reena says, "Ok mere old father". It was not that Kishore Das did

not love his wife Sarada Das. And there was a lot of sorrow for him and why not both of them had done love marriage in that era too. Kishore Das used to go to the shop with his father and Reena used to stay at the flower shop of his house. Both were in front of each other and then what was the matter, both of them fell in love and then married. This journey started from the same flower shop and finally ended on flowers. Now only Kishore Das is left and Reena is a story of Sarada Das and Kishore Das's love.

"Oh this morning - in the morning I thought that you have forgotten that you have a friend too," Reena says with a cry seeing her friend Bhavna coming home.

“What do you guys have time to come to this site?” Bhavna says while keeping her shopping bag in her hand on a pedestal.

“Namaste Uncle” looks at Kishore Das, says Bhavna.

Kishore Das, "Hello son, tell me everything is fine at home"

"Yes uncle, everything is fine" the feeling goes away.

"Come on, both of you friends talk about me, if it's time to go to the shop, then I will go," Kishore Das says and then leaves from there.

"Man, I heard about Sarada aunty, I felt very bad," Bhavna says with a slight sadness.

Rina, "Now you can do in front of God's choice,"

Reena's face to know speaks of change Bhavana thing was so sad you tomorrow boy Are I see thought this was it was taking clothes today for Let me tell you to come in front too.

"What? Means you are getting married" says Reena choking.

"Hmm"

"Wah man, I wish you a good husband," Reena says with a smile.

"And congratulations to you too, my dear, I have heard that you have got a college to become a doctor," Bhavna says to Reena.

Reena, "Yes right, you have heard."

"Hey wa give me a magic hug, I am very happy that your dream is about to come true" Bhavna is embracing Reena.

"These Muna Bhai dialogs don't stop killing them till now" Reena speaks with emotion.

After sitting for some time, both of them talked, and then the call started coming from Bhavna's house that she had not come to the house after telling that she would also meet Reena. And Bhavna leaves from there. Bhavna leaves by telling Reena to come to her wedding.

Reena's scooty had also arrived for a few days and in the meantime, Reena had also

learned to drive it with the help of a friend of her locality.

First day---

of collegeToday is Reena's first day of college and Reena wearing a blue jeans and a red color topper is sitting on her scooty then Kishore Das tells Reena to go comfortably wearing a helmet |

Reena starts her scooty and leaves for college. Neither she had any friends nor Reena knew anyone, all the children were reaching the class, but Reena

did not understand where to sit, only then she hears a voice, "First day is of college." Reena looks back. So there was a girl standing. Reena sees him and says "yes" then that girl comes to Reena and says "Hello I am Akrati"shaking

Reenahands "Reena, I am Reena Das"

Let's go to class then Aarti speaks.

Reena, "I don't even know where the class is"

"I know come with me" Aarti speaks to Reena.

In both the classes, she sits on the same bench. In the class comes Professor Ramakant who introduces him to all the children. Akrati and Reena share their numbers with each other. Seeing the wallpaper of her mother Sarada on Reena's phone, Akrati asks, "This is your mommy"

Reena, "Yes, she passed away a few months ago and this phone is her last Nisani, I have some pictures of her in it. I lighten up

"I have passed you mean" Akrati asks Reena.

"Blood cancer was them," Reena says.

As the days passed by, Reena and Akrati's friendship started deepening. Reena goes to college everyday and comes home. On the other hand, Kishore Das had also started home delivery at his shop. Once when Kishore Das had fallen ill, it was Reena who started taking care of the shop. There was a delivery guy who used to deliver whatever orders came in.

The sky was getting cloudy that day and it was almost eight

o'clock in the night. Reena was about to close the shop when a call came from a customer and he orders a cake. When I saw the boy delivering Reena's knee, he could not find it and had gone home till now. Then Reena herself goes away with the order. Going there and sees that there is a lady who made the order, the age was about 40 years old. When Reena came back after giving orders, it had started raining, so where did that lady ask Reena to sit in the house for some time? Reena also agrees to him and goes to

his house. Both of them sat down and started talking after a long time, when the rain stopped, Reena starts leaving from there, only then she gives her number to Lady Reena and says that there is a job for you to talk on these numbers. After a few days, that lady called Reena and called to meet. out Reena also reached to meet where that lady had asked to come.

Next Subha Kishore Das gets a call that the police have found Reena's dead body in a deserted vacant house outside the city.

Kishore Das suddenly falls unconscious on hearing this. And report to the police. Reena had told that she was going to meet some lady, Kishore Das got the report done against her. The police got the lady's number from Reena's phone and called her to Thane. The next morning the hearing of the case was in the court and both Kishore Das's lawyer and defense's lawyer presented their arguments. The defense alleged that Kishore Das used to get Reena to work, that is why he finally committed suicide after

getting fed up with the car. Then based on evidence and statements, for getting child labor done, he was sentenced to one year according to section 14.

Indhar Mathur read the letter containing that parcel and at the end, it was also written that

"I am that Reena who is dead but my soul is still wandering waiting for justice. I want you to reopen my case"

"And I have chosen you because the lawyer who fought this case

was none other than your father Mohan Mathur from the defense side. That's why this is you too that you can also take your revenge."

chance forIndhar Mathur was waiting for this day to get a case that he could give Mohan Mathur a taste of defeat. Then Indra Mathur applies for reopening Reena's case the very next morning and as soon as this thing comes into the media, it was just being discussed all around, everyone was waiting whether a son would be able to give a necklace to his father. |

Indra Mathur meets Kishore Das in jail and finds out about everything.

Today was a very special day for Indhar Mathur because today after so many years he was going to fight a case in front of his father. There was a lot of enthusiasm in the media too, everyone was waiting for that finally who wins and will Reena get justice?

Both the lawyers had arrived in the court and the proceedings of the case had started. The statements of both the

Ghwavos were taken. Defense lawyer Mohan Mathur was seen winning so far when Indhar Mathur sought permission to show a video in the court. The judge granted the permission and the video plays. In the video, Reena and her hands are being seen by many people who are in the same room, all are taken on different beds and some doctors are doing their tests. Then the video ends and Indra Mathur starts talking about it.

Indhar Mathur says that this video is of a research lab where people have been made test

subjects and a new drug clinical trial is going on on them and this is a foreign pharma industry doing the trial. Who do clinical trials in India because here greedy people like this lady doctor are found, who push their people into the face of death, BS for some money. Now I request the court that this lady should be punished severely and my client MR. Kishore Das ji should be released.

That doctor is sentenced to life imprisonment and Indhar Mathur had a dream, that too is fulfilled. After this case, Indhar

Mathur earns more name than his father Mohan Mathur, but after this Mohan Mathur realizes his mistake and leaves the practice.

Thanks Letter

thanks to you for reading this book.

9 798885 695206

Printed by Libri Plureos GmbH in Hamburg, Germany